D1277313

Poinciana Christian Church
4900 Pleasant Hill Road
Kissimmee, Florida 34759
870-9700

What Happened to A.J.?

A STORY ABOUT HUMAN RIGHTS

Written by
JOY BERRY

WORD INC.
Waco, Texas 76796

About the Author and Publisher

Joy Berry's mission in life is to help families cope with everyday problems and to help children become competent, responsible, happy individuals. To achieve her goal, she has written over two hundred self-help books for children from birth through age twelve. Her work revolutionized children's publishing by providing families with practical, how-to, living skills information that was previously unavailable in children's books.

Joy gathered a dedicated team of experts, including psychologists, educators, child developmentalists, writers, designers, and artists, to form her publishing company and to help produce her work.

The company, Living Skills Press, produces thoroughly researched books and audio-visual materials that successfully combine humor and education to teach subjects ranging from how to clean a bedroom to how to resolve problems and get along with other people.

Copyright © 1987 by Joy Berry
Living Skills Press, Sebastopol, CA
All rights reserved.
Printed in the United States of America.

Managing Editor: Ellen Klarberg
Copy Editor: Kate Dickey
Contributing Editors: Marilyn Berry, Libby Byers,
Donna Fisher, Michael McBride, Gretchen Savidge
Editorial Assistant: Sandy Passarino

Art Director: Laurie Westdahl
Design: Laurie Westdahl
Production: Caroline Rennard
Illustration design: Bartholomew
Inker: Susie Hornig
Colorer: Susie Hornig
Composition: Dwan Typography

Published by Word Incorporated in cooperation with Living Skills Press.

Hello, my name is Joy, and I'd like to tell you a story about A.J.'s family and the important lesson they learned about human rights and responsibilities.

Tami and T.J. raced to the living room window just in time to see a police car turn into the driveway. The policeman's arrival added to the tension that was already present in the Jones household.

Mr. and Mrs. Jones had been extremely upset all evening, and even though they weren't admitting it, the children knew something was seriously wrong.

"He's here!" T.J. yelled as he raced to the front door.

"I'm going to open the door!" Tami demanded.

T.J. shouted, "Not if I get there first!"

Mrs. Jones rushed into the hallway where the kids were struggling to push each other away from the front door.

"Neither of you is going to open the door!" Mrs. Jones snapped nervously as she led both children into the living room.

Carl, the only teenager in the Jones family, seemed totally oblivious to everything that was happening around him. He was stretched out on the living room couch, guzzling down a soda and watching TV.

Carl considered himself to be "entirely too mature" to be affected by anything short of a tornado.

At the moment, the only thing bothering Carl was Tami and T.J.'s continued bickering, which was drowning out the sounds of his TV program.

"You guys have got to be pretty hard up if the high point of your day is opening the front door! Keep it down, would you?"

For most of the evening, Mrs. Jones had done a fairly good job of keeping her emotions under control. But seeing her older son's obvious lack of concern was more than she could handle.

"Carl, this is no time for you to be teasing Tami and T.J. I need you to help me get them ready for bed."

Carl heaved a big sigh while Tami and T.J. protested.

"We want to see the policeman."

"Why do *we* always have to go to bed while *everyone* else gets to stay up?"

By this time, Mr. Jones had answered the doorbell and had invited the policeman into the house.

Forgetting everything else, Mrs. Jones rushed to her husband's side.

Tami and T.J. looked at each other gleefully. They knew that when their mother was distracted she would completely forget she had asked anyone to do anything. They also knew Carl would act as though he had not heard his parents ask him to do something. It took at least three reminders and a lot of yelling to get Carl to complete even the simplest task.

T.J. whispered to Tami, "Mom and Dad won't get mad at us while the policeman is here!"

"You're probably right, but if they *do*, we'll tell them we're waiting for Carl to help us," Tami whispered back.

It looked as though circumstances were helping the children win the bedtime battle for the time being. However, both Tami and T.J. knew that they had better not press their luck! They would have to be "totally good" so no one would notice them if they were going to stay up past their bedtime.

"We're really sorry to have to bother you," Mr. Jones told the policeman.

Mrs. Jones added, "It's just that our son A.J. is not the kind of child to be away from home for *this* long."

The policeman responded sympathetically, "You don't have to apologize. When a child is missing, it's the police department's job to help the parents find that child."

The three adults walked into the living room, and Mr.
Jones motioned to Carl to turn off the TV.

Carl grudgingly pressed the "off" button on the TV's
remote control.

Tami's and T.J.'s eyes widened as the policeman walked past them. They had never been *that* close to a police officer before. Neither one of them could stop staring at all the neat stuff that was dangling from his belt. There was a walkie-talkie, a can of mace, some handcuffs, a billy club, some bullets, and . . . a gun!

"I wonder if he ever had to shoot his gun at anyone," T.J. whispered to Tami.

"I don't know, but this is the first time I've ever seen a *real* gun!" Tami whispered back.

As the policeman began filling out the "missing persons" report attached to his clipboard, even Carl began to sense the seriousness of the situation. He tried to act casually about the whole thing, but as the policeman questioned his mom and dad, he found it more and more difficult to hide his growing concern.

The policeman continued, "Mr. and Mrs. Jones, look, you've done all the right things. You've checked out A.J.'s favorite hangouts. You've called all of his friends. But tell me, can you think of any reason why A.J. might want to run away?"

"Did A.J. run away?" T.J. blurted out.
Tami chimed in, "Is he never coming back?"

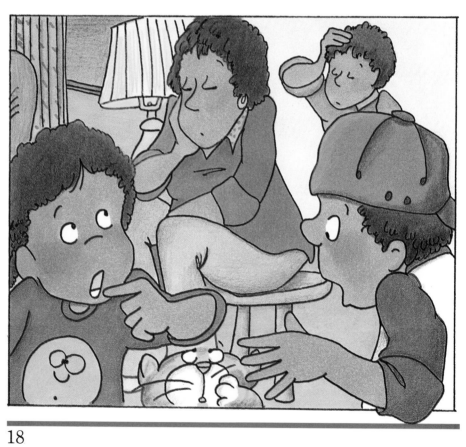

Mrs. Jones motioned for the children to come sit by her while Mr. Jones said, "Now let's not jump to conclusions. A.J. is going to be just fine."

For some reason, Mr. Jones' words did not sound convincing. Tami and T.J. scurried over to their mother and nestled close to her.

The excitement that surrounded the policeman's visit was overshadowed by the fact that A.J. was really gone!
Was he lost?
Had he been kidnapped?
Now Tami and T.J. were getting scared too!

For the first time Carl talked to the policeman.

"I don't know if this is anything worth mentioning, but . . . A.J. belongs to this group called the Human Race Club, and he's always doing weird things like . . . well, like last week he came home from a club meeting and started working on this poster. You know the one I'm talking about, don't you, Mom?"

Mrs. Jones looked puzzled for a moment and then spoke up.

"Do you mean the one that listed human rights?"

Carl continued, "Yeah, that's the one. Well, anyway, he took the thing so seriously! Remember how he kept bugging everyone about having a family meeting to talk about our rights? He kept saying weird things like, 'We don't respect each other's rights.' You know, that really bothered him."

Just then Tami jumped to her feet and interrupted Carl. "I know the poster you're talking about! It's the one T.J. scribbled all over!"

T.J. protested, "Hey, big mouth! Let's not forget that you scribbled on it too!"

Mr. Jones gave Tami and T.J. a look that said, "Don't interrupt while someone else is talking."

Remembering it was long past their bedtime, the two children settled down immediately.

Carl continued, "Yeah, A.J. was pretty upset about Tami and T.J. ruining his poster. But even more than that, he felt bad because he couldn't get anyone to listen to him."

"Carl, did he talk about running away?" the policeman asked.

Carl thought for a moment and then answered, "You know, come to think of it, he did! Last night, just before he went to bed, he said something like, 'No one should have to live with people who don't respect each other's rights.'"

Carl's words made it impossible for Mrs. Jones to hold back her tears.

Tami and T.J. felt uncomfortable seeing their mother cry. They had never seen her *this* upset before.

Mr. Jones reached over and gently took his wife's hand.

It was quiet for a moment, and then Mr. Jones spoke, "Everyone is going to be OK. A.J. is coming back, and when he does, things are going to be different around here. You know, A.J. is right. We *should* be more respectful of each other's rights! And besides . . ."

Mr. Jones rambled on and on. He always tended to do that whenever he was nervous or upset. Mrs. Jones nodded her head in agreement, but she was finding it hard to concentrate on what her husband was saying.

The policeman had all the information he needed. After promising to put out an all-points bulletin announcing the fact that A.J. was missing, he left through the same door he had entered.

Minutes after the policeman had gone, the doorbell rang for the second time that evening. This time everyone, including Carl, rushed to the front door.

When Mr. Jones finally opened the door, the entire family stood looking at the policeman who had taken their report. He had a grin on his face that went from ear to ear.

"Does this young man look familiar?"
The policeman stepped aside to reveal a bedraggled boy standing behind him.

"A.J.!" Tami and T.J. yelled.

Mr. and Mrs. Jones threw their arms around A.J. and held him close as the policeman continued to talk to them.

"I found him down the street, walking home. I think A.J. discovered that running away from home isn't all it's cracked up to be."

Carl was relieved to see that A.J. was OK. But of course it wouldn't be "cool" to let anyone know how he felt.

Mr. and Mrs. Jones thanked the policeman, and the whole family waved good-bye as he drove away.

Back inside the house, Mr. Jones spoke sternly to A.J.

"We've got a lot to talk about, A.J., but right now all of us need to get some rest."

A.J. stared at the floor. He wasn't looking forward to the "talk" his dad referred to, but other than that, he was glad to be home.

Getting into a nice warm bed sounded good to A.J. and, surprisingly enough, it sounded good to Tami and T.J. as well.

Carl pushed open the door to A.J.'s room and leaned inside. It was dark and quiet.

"Hey, man, wasn't one of the rights on your poster, 'The right to live free from fear?'" Carl asked.

There was a pause, and then A.J. responded, "Yeah!"

"Well, did it ever occur to you that *you* were not respecting other people's rights when you ran away? You had everyone in this family pretty scared, you know!" Carl said.

A.J. didn't answer. But, as Carl closed the door and walked down the hall, he knew A.J. was smiling.

So what can we learn from all of this?

A.J. learned the hard way that running away from home is not a good way to resolve family problems.

There are several things A.J. could have done to make things go a little more smoothly.

What A.J. wanted to accomplish with his family was too important to be ignored. A.J. needed the cooperation of his parents to do what he wanted to do.

To make sure his parents listened to him, A.J. should have talked to them at a time when they were not distracted. He should have set up a time during which his parents could give him their full attention.

Once a time had been established, A.J. should have waited patiently for that time to come and not bothered his parents while he waited.

There are a lot of people in A.J.'s family. Sometimes it can be tough to get that many people together to discuss something.

A.J. should not have given up when the family meeting didn't take place.

If he couldn't deal with the group as a whole, he could have turned his effort to the individuals in the group.

Talking with people one at a time can be just as effective as talking to people in a group.

Sometimes people don't listen to what you have to say. This is especially true of the people in your family.

When people won't listen to you, you should communicate with them in other ways. One of the most effective ways to communicate with people is through your actions.

If you behave like a person who is worthy of respect and if you treat others respectfully, you can teach the people around you a lot about human rights.

EPILOG

I talked with A.J. soon after his "running-away-from-home" episode. I shared with him the information about communication that I just shared with you.

The other day I went to A.J.'s house to pick him up for a club meeting. A.J. said at that time that things were getting better. He didn't give me any of the details, but he didn't have to . . . I saw the human rights poster he had made hanging on the refrigerator door, scribbles and all.

The End